THE SORCERER'S APPRENTICE

TED DEWAN

PICTURE CORGI BOOKS

IN RECOGNITION
OF THE TORMENTED
APPRENTICESHIP
SERVED BY
ALL YOUNGER
BROTHERS
THIS BOOK
ALONG WITH THE
M U S I C
IS DEDICATED TO
B R I A N

Not far away, and not so long ago, there lived a brilliant inventor. His workshop was full of strange and wonderful machines...

...like the Blonkwhirler,
the Trachett-spink,
and the Zumtubber.

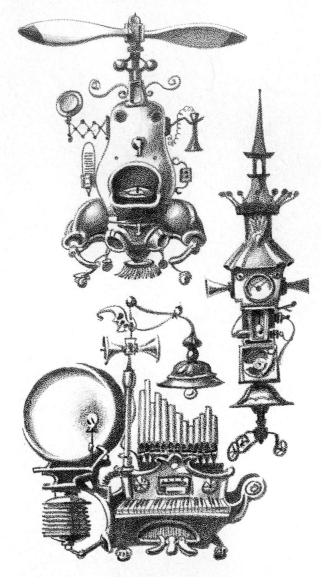

Everyone thought the inventor's
machines were magical, so they
called him the Sorcerer.

The Sorcerer spent all his time on his inventions, so he never had time to clean up. The harder he worked, the messier his workshop became; until one day, he couldn't find the way out. "What a mess!" he cried. "If only these machines could pick up after themselves!"

Then he had a clever idea. "A robot!" he shouted. "That's what I need to clean up my workshop. I'll build myself a robot right now."

First, the Sorcerer drew up some plans. Then he rooted about, scooping up tubes, wires and gears. All day long, he fiddled and twiddled and tweaked...

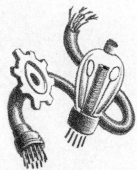

...then the other foot went bump...

...and the Sorcerer's Apprentice came to life.

"Magic! It works!" cheered the Sorcerer.

The Apprentice blinked in reply.

"Look here, little buddy," said the Sorcerer, "I need some help around here. First I'll teach you how to use your vacuum cleaner."

The Apprentice learned fast, and the Sorcerer was as pleased as punch.

"Now, I want you to tidy up until your battery runs down," said the Sorcerer. "Tomorrow, I'll recharge you and maybe teach you a few tricks, OK?"

The Sorcerer yawned good-night and went off to bed.

But the Apprentice's day was only just beginning.

The Apprentice snatched the Sorcerer's hat off the post and put it on his head. "Whee! Look at me!" he sang, and twirled around the workshop. But something caught his eye and he stopped to take a closer look. "Hey, this is a picture of me!" he said.

Then the Apprentice had a clever idea. "I can build myself a robot with these plans - and then it can do my chores for me!" Soon he was scooping up tubes and wires and gears. He fiddled and twiddled and tweaked.

When the Apprentice had finally finished, he put a disc in the copy robot's head. Remembering the Sorcerer's magic words, he said:

PRESTO VIVACE,
TREMOLO WHEEL!
BRING TO LIFE
THIS HEAD OF STEEL!

The new robot spun around and stomped through the workshop.

"Magic! It works!" shouted the Apprentice. He wobbled off to find a cosy place to recharge his tired battery.

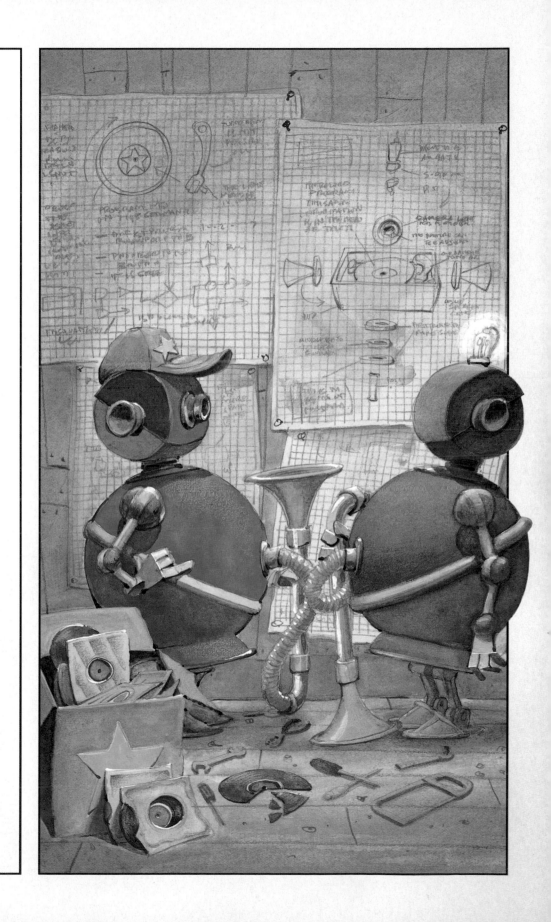

Back in the workshop, it didn't take long for the copy robot to have a clever idea once it noticed the Sorcerer's plans...

...and soon another robot was finished...

Of course, each robot thought exactly the same way as the last, so they just kept on copying themselves.

The two robots multiplied into four...

then eight...

then sixteen....

Soon there were dozens of robots, frantically rooting around for parts to make more copies...

...until all the tubes and wires and gears were used up.

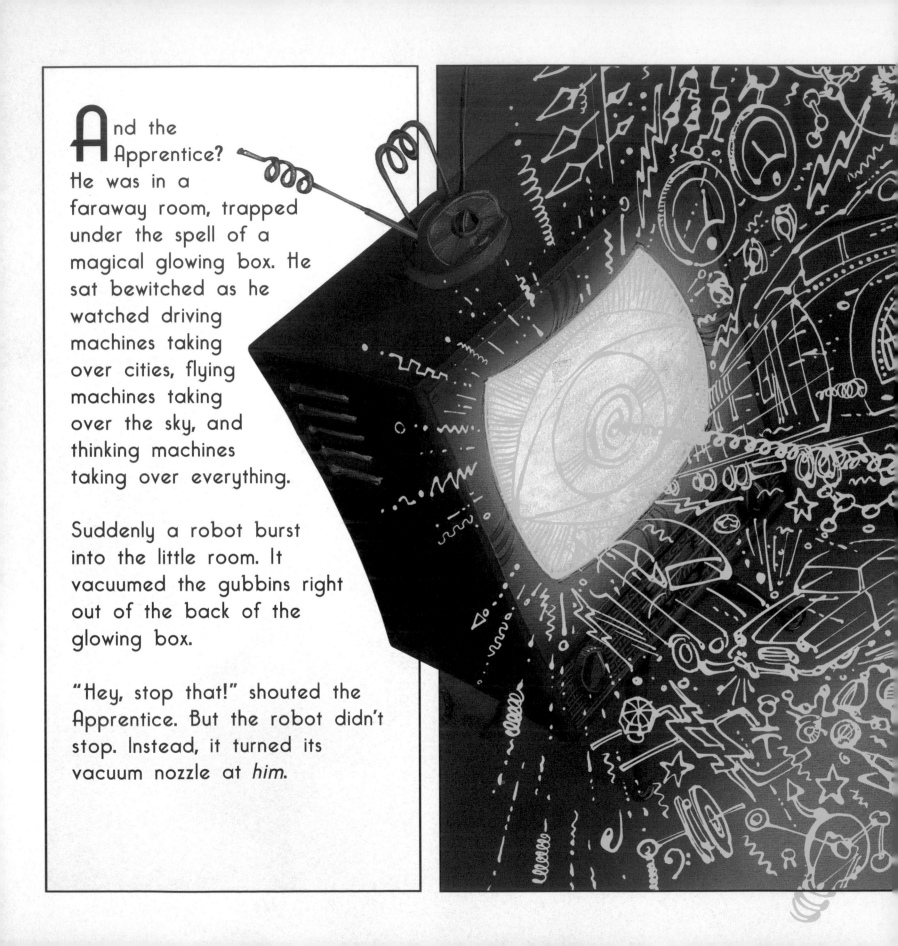

And the Apprentice? He was in a faraway room, trapped under the spell of a magical glowing box. He sat bewitched as he watched driving machines taking over cities, flying machines taking over the sky, and thinking machines taking over everything.

Suddenly a robot burst into the little room. It vacuumed the gubbins right out of the back of the glowing box.

"Hey, stop that!" shouted the Apprentice. But the robot didn't stop. Instead, it turned its vacuum nozzle at *him*.

"Leave me alone, idiot!" yelped the Apprentice. Terrified, he swung his nozzle at the robot, and with a CRACK he whacked the robot's head right off.

And all went quiet.

"Crazy junk-pile," said the Apprentice. Then he noticed a low buzzing sound.

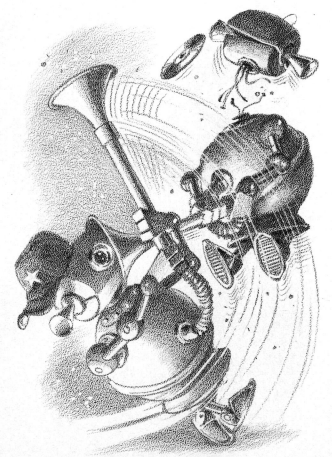

Step by step, the Apprentice crept down a long hallway. The buzzing got louder and louder as he neared the workshop doors. He flung the doors open and was stunned by what he saw...

There was a great ARMY of robots. They had torn up the workshop and were all buzzing full of electricity.

"Yipes!" squeaked the Apprentice. "What's going on here?"

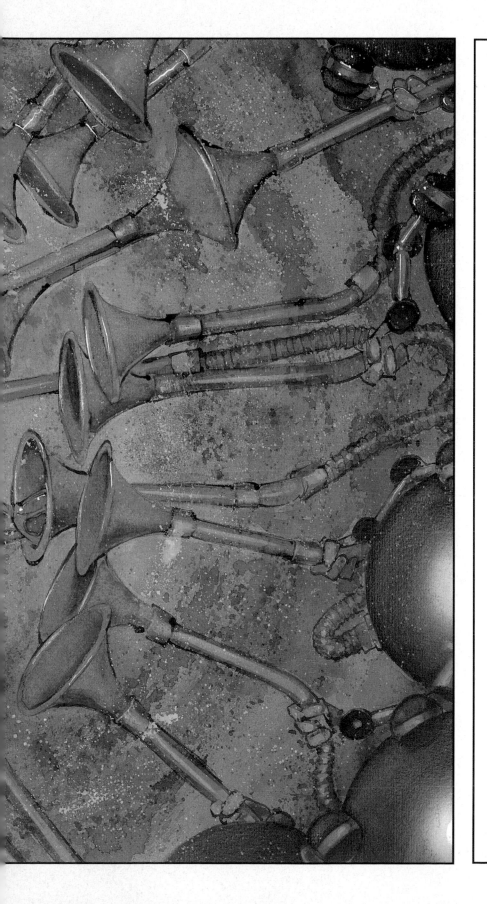

The robots spun their heads towards the Apprentice. They surrounded him. They raised their nozzles. They switched on, and their powerful vacuums began to suck.

"Help!" the Apprentice howled. "They're tearing me apart! HELP ME!"

The Sorcerer leapt out of bed and ran to the workshop. "Holy smoke," he cried. "Hold on, little buddy!"

The Sorcerer grabbed hold of the emergency power switch. He pulled down the huge handle. And with an almighty

BUZZZ!

CRACKLE!

KaBOOM!

...the robots were blown to bits.

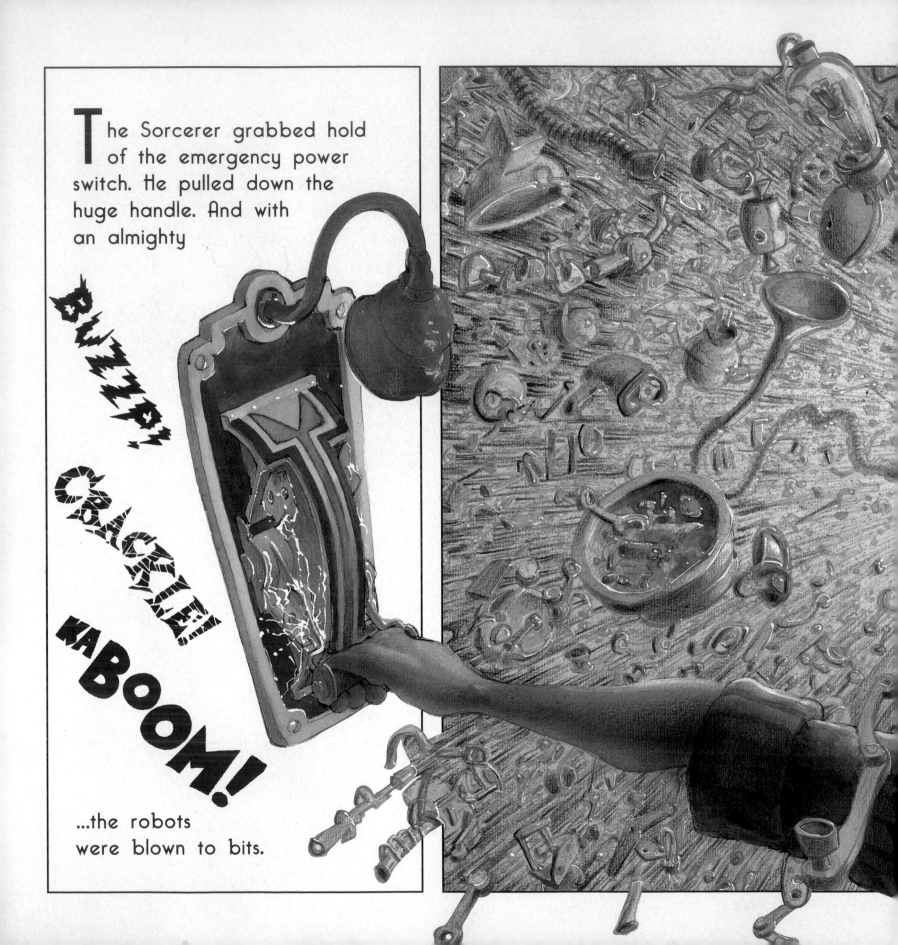

The Sorcerer blinked.

The Apprentice blinked back.

"Well little buddy," said the Sorcerer, "it looks like your machines got out of control and took control of *you*. Come on, I'll make you a nice hot cup of oil, and then we'll clean up this mess together."

From that night onwards, the Apprentice was eager to learn at the Sorcerer's side. And he was especially careful not to fool around with things he didn't understand...

...most of the time.

A PICTURE CORGI BOOK: 0 552 545287

First published in Great Britain by Doubleday, a division of Transworld Publishers Ltd

PRINTING HISTORY
Doubleday edition published 1997
Picture Corgi edition published 1998

Picture Corgi Books are published by Transworld Publishers Ltd,
61-63 Uxbridge Road, Ealing, London W5 5SA,
in Australia by Transworld Publishers (Australia) Pty. Ltd,
15-25 Helles Avenue, Moorebank, NSW 2170,
and in New Zealand by Transworld Publishers (NZ) Ltd,
3 William Pickering Drive, Albany, Auckland.

Printed in Belgium by Proost